ALL UPON A
SIDEWALK

ALL UPON A SIDEWALK

by Jean Craighead George

illustrated by Don Bolognese

E. P. Dutton & Co., Inc.   New York

Text copyright © 1974 by Jean Craighead George
Illustrations copyright © 1974 by Don Bolognese

LIBRARY OF CONGRESS CATALOGING IN PUBLICATION DATA

George, Jean Craighead   All upon a sidewalk.

SUMMARY: Relates the experiences of a city-dwelling ant
as she seeks sugar for the ant community.

1. Lasius flavus — Juvenile literature. [1. Ants]
I. Bolognese, Don, illus. II. Title.
QL568.F7G37   595.7′96   74-5229   ISBN 0-525-25462-5

Published simultaneously in Canada by Clarke,
Irwin & Company Limited, Toronto and Vancouver

Designed by Meri Shardin
Printed in the U.S.A.   First Edition

10 9 8 7 6 5 4 3 2 1

This book is dedicated to:

Phylum Arthropoda
Class Insecta
Order Hymenoptera
Family Formicidae
Genus Lasius
Species flavus
or
Lasius flavus, the common yellow ant

From:

Jean Craighead George, Homo sapiens

The sun came over the curve of the earth, lit up the city, and awakened the wild things on 19th Street.

A sparrow yawned, a cricket chirped, and Lasius flavus peered out of her doorway in a crack in the sidewalk.

She was a yellow ant with big eyes, narrow waist, and a glittering assortment of six spindly legs.

Her apartment-like home lay under the sidewalk. It had corridors, pantries, nurseries, and other rooms. There were barns for the ant cows—little turtle-shaped scale bugs and humped-back aphids.

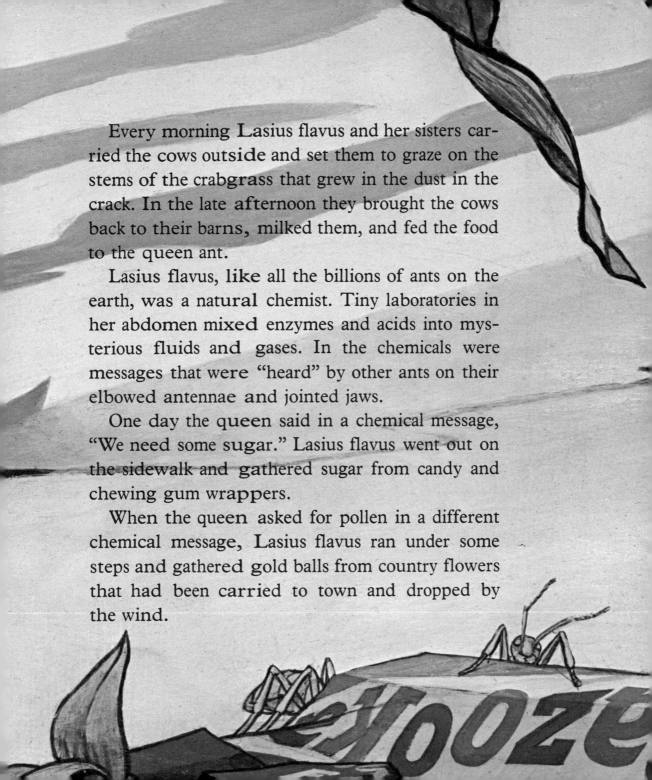

Every morning Lasius flavus and her sisters carried the cows outside and set them to graze on the stems of the crabgrass that grew in the dust in the crack. In the late afternoon they brought the cows back to their barns, milked them, and fed the food to the queen ant.

Lasius flavus, like all the billions of ants on the earth, was a natural chemist. Tiny laboratories in her abdomen mixed enzymes and acids into mysterious fluids and gases. In the chemicals were messages that were "heard" by other ants on their elbowed antennae and jointed jaws.

One day the queen said in a chemical message, "We need some sugar." Lasius flavus went out on the sidewalk and gathered sugar from candy and chewing gum wrappers.

When the queen asked for pollen in a different chemical message, Lasius flavus ran under some steps and gathered gold balls from country flowers that had been carried to town and dropped by the wind.

Today, however, Lasius flavus did not know where to go. The queen had asked for a wondrous treasure called Euplectus confluens. It was terribly appealing, and hidden somewhere in the city. Lasius flavus had but one clue—a taste of Euplectus. The queen had acquired it in some food from the sidewalk, but where it had come from the ants did not know.

Lasius flavus climbed out of the crack and scanned the vast desert before her. The sidewalk, to her, was pitted with craters; each sand grain was a rock, each pebble a boulder. The cracks were canyons.

Lasius flavus took to the highway her sisters had built with layers of chemicals. She found nothing appealing along its course, just carbon from cars and oil from the street. She stepped into a groove made long ago by the sidewalk maker's cement trowel. The groove was carpeted with a tiny green moss. It grew from dusty seed spores that floated in the air and came down to the sidewalk in droplets of rain.

As she walked along, she laid down a chemical trail of her own so she could find her way back home.

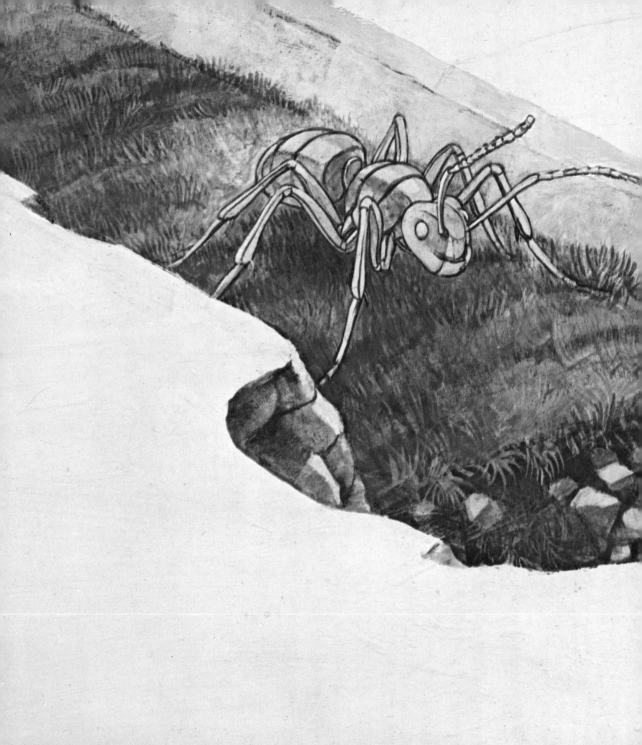

Far down the groove she came to a cave made by a stone that had been pried out of the cement by the ice of winter. A spider lurked in it.

The spider had sailed into the cave on a long thread of silk she had spun from her body after hatching from her egg. She had flown over the treetops, over the river, and around the buildings to 19th Street. Reefing in on her sail, she had steered herself to the cave near the ant house. There she was ready to trap ants that came down the groove. An evil chemical poured from the cave, warning Lasius flavus not to go on. She scrambled quickly out of the groove!

A dark cloud loomed on the sidewalk. Lasius flavus pulled down her antennae and lowered her head as a dust storm struck. Pollen from the pines in the park, fungi spores from the wood in old buildings, sand, soot, and dust whirled around her. She tested each scent; but none was appealing.

Climbing up on a bottle cap, she listened with all her six ears that lay like drumheads on the sides of her body. A migrating swallow called from the sky. A mountainous taxi roared down the street.

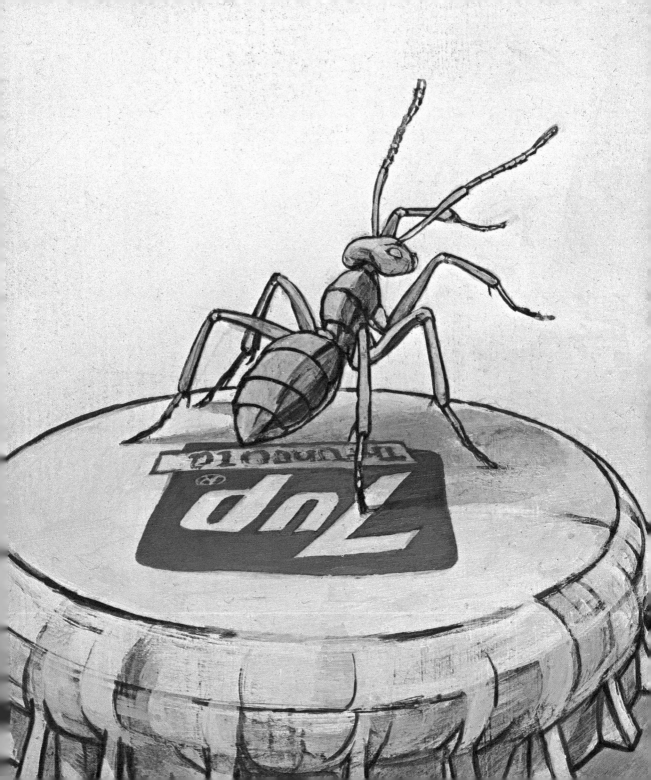

Lasius flavus turned in another direction. Wings whistled and whined. A fruit bee was coming her way as it languidly cruised above the 19th Street sidewalk.

Lasius flavus stood up on her two back feet, opened her jaws, and picked up the scent from the bee. It was sweet with the juice of a pear it had sipped at the fruit stand.

But it was **not** *appealing*.

The treasure-seeking Lasius flavus was not even tempted to follow the bee. Instead she climbed down from the bottle cap and walked gingerly out on the huge, endless sidewalk.

Suddenly her hard outer coat tightened against her body. She knew what this meant! The air pressure was dropping, a rain storm was coming. She wheeled on all six feet and hastened her gait.

She zigged toward a building to investigate a rumble. It was only the roots of a wall pepper plant bulldozing into the dust by the building. The plant had sprung from a seed that had been brought to the sidewalk in the droppings of a bird.

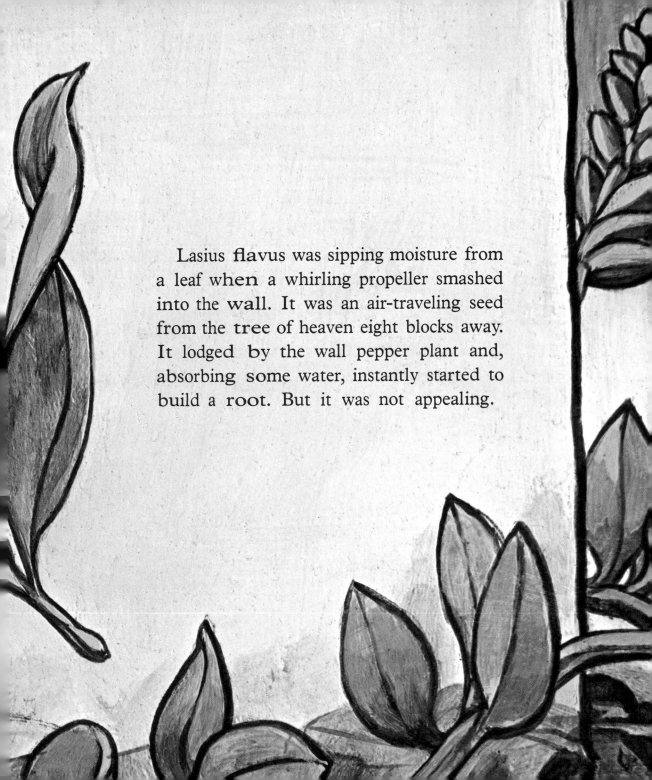

Lasius flavus was sipping moisture from a leaf when a whirling propeller smashed into the wall. It was an air-traveling seed from the tree of heaven eight blocks away. It lodged by the wall pepper plant and, absorbing some water, instantly started to build a root. But it was not appealing.

People were passing. Their footfalls made cyclones. Lasius flavus ran into a soda straw.

In a calm she dashed for the curb. A boot slammed to the sidewalk and gusted her under the cellophane wrapper from a cigarette pack. She climbed into it, looking for something appealing, just as a sparrow picked up the wrapper.

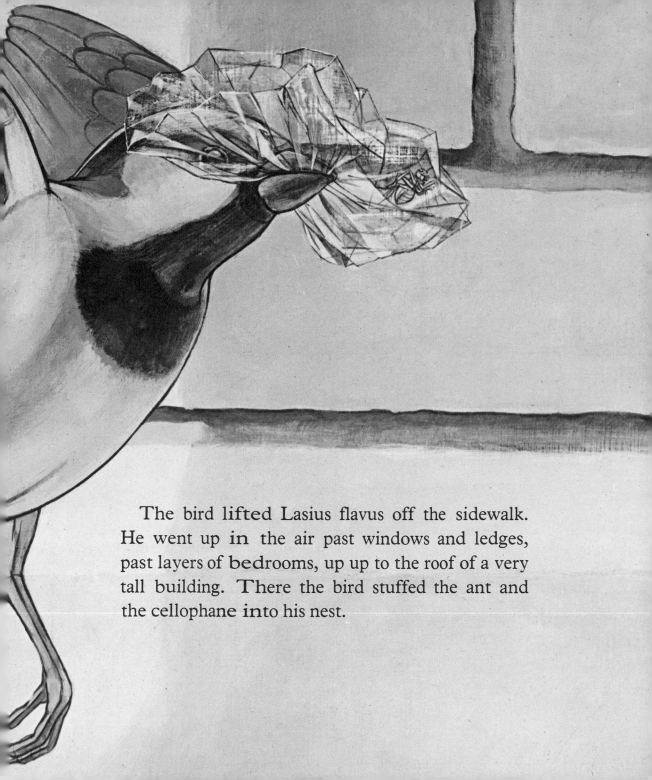

The bird lifted Lasius flavus off the sidewalk.
He went up in the air past windows and ledges,
past layers of bedrooms, up up to the roof of a very
tall building. There the bird stuffed the ant and
the cellophane into his nest.

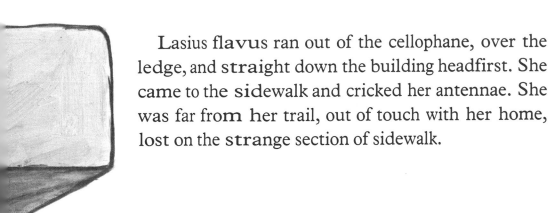

Lasius flavus ran out of the cellophane, over the ledge, and straight down the building headfirst. She came to the sidewalk and cricked her antennae. She was far from her trail, out of touch with her home, lost on the strange section of sidewalk.

Quickly Lasius flavus began to circle wider and wider as she looked for her trail. She found a snail egg that had dropped off the toe of a pigeon who had just returned from the riverbank. She found a watch beetle that lives in the wood of doors, windowsills, tables, and benches.

But she did not find her trail!

Desperately she circled this way and that, rounded the corner, and stepped onto the highway of the avenue ants. Lasius flavus spun her antennae, walked on her hind legs, darted and zagged. On *this* highway there was something appealing.

It grew stronger and stronger as she followed the trail, up a step, up a flowerpot, and into the home of the avenue ants. The avenue ants lived around the corner from Lasius flavus in the shade of bright petunia plants.

Lasius flavus stopped running. A pit lay before her, the deep dark shaft of an earthworm's home. Suddenly a mammoth fire engine thundered down the avenue. The flowerpot rocked. The dry earth crumbled, and Lasius flavus fell into the pit.

Dirt poured on her head. The worm hole collapsed and opened a wall into the home of the avenue ants.

In the rubble and debris was something appealing! Lasius flavus threw back the stones. There in the dust sat Euplectus confluens, an insect known as the ant-loving beetle. The treasure was found.

The beetle opened his mouth and stuck out his tongue. It was broad and exactly fitted the contours of her face. With a soft lick he said, "Please feed me." Lasius flavus stuffed him with food from her body. As she did so, the yellow hairs on his back turned into fountains. From them an exotic drink welled up that tasted like flowers and gardens and herbs.

When Lasius flavus had drunk from the fountains, the ant-loving beetle held out his antenna. It was shaped to exactly fit the joints of her mouth. Lasius flavus closed her jaws on the knob and picked up Euplectus as if he were a little frying pan.

The soil rumbled. The avenue ants were coming after her.

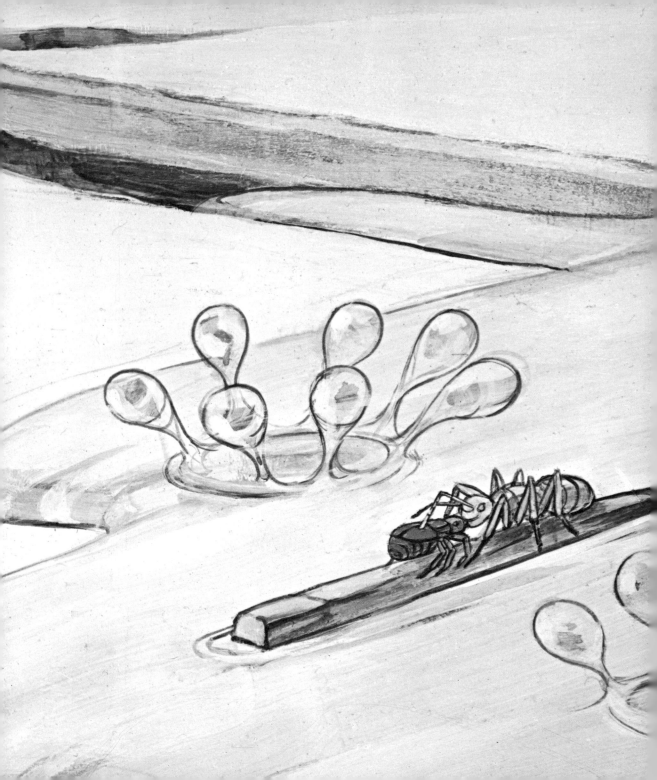

They wanted their beetle back! Lasius ran up the worm hole, around the flower stems, and down to the sidewalk. The avenue ants swarmed out of the flowerpot. But Lasius flavus turned off her trail-making chemicals as she rounded the corner. Now there was no way for the other ants to track her. But where was her own trail? She was lost on a prairie of cement. The wind blew, raindrops splashed and formed little lakes. The lakes joined together and created a sea. Lasius flavus climbed up on a match-stick. The sea became an ocean, the matchstick a boat. Lasius flavus and the ant-loving beetle sailed down the sidewalk.

They rammed into a bottle cap, fell off the match-stick, and were pulled by the current far under the water. They spun into a cave made safe by a bubble of air. But it was also the lair of the spider!

The spider opened her jaws. Two poison fangs rolled out.

Instantly Lasius flavus brewed up a chemical. She laid a foul-smelling wall around herself and the ant-loving beetle. The spider backed up and crawled deep into her cave.

The rain stopped, the ocean sank, and Lasius flavus looked out at the sun. She picked up her treasure and scampered up the groove. Her highway was gone, washed away by the rain. Using her eyes, she found her way past familiar craters.

Finally she came to the edge of her crack. Her door was not there. It had been crushed by the flood. Lasius flavus drooped her antennae. Her spindly legs collapsed at the joints. She sank to her belly as the ant-loving beetle turned on his fountains —a delicious message went out!

Sand rumbled, dust heaved, and up from the sidewalk came some of her sisters. They pushed up the sand, opened the door, and welcomed the treasure and Lasius home.

All the pictures in this book, depicting the world of Lasius flavus, are contained in these three paintings. Mr. Bolognese developed the technique for an earlier book by Jean George, *All Upon a Stone*.

JEAN CRAIGHEAD GEORGE is the author of many books on the Dutton list, including *My Side of the Mountain* (Newbery Medal Honor Book) and *Who Really Killed Cock Robin? Julie of the Wolves* (Harper & Row) received the 1973 Newbery Medal. Jean George is also a Roving Editor for the *Reader's Digest*. Prior to her exploration of the world of *All Upon a Sidewalk*, she and Don Bolognese worked together on *All Upon a Stone* (T. Y. Crowell), which received the 1971 picture book award of the Book World Spring Book Festival.

DON BOLOGNESE has illustrated more than a hundred books, including two recent titles that he also wrote, *Challenge for a Rookie* and *A New Day*. Mr. Bolognese was trained at Cooper Union. He has taught there and at Pratt Institute and New York University. He and his family divide their time between Vermont and New York City. His research for *All Upon a Sidewalk* was done from life—getting down on his hands and knees to look at the sidewalk environment through a magnifying glass.

The display type is set in Patina and the text type in Plantin. The full-color paintings were done in acrylics on gesso wood panels. The book was printed by offset at Pearl Pressman Liberty.